Rudolph

to the Rescue

Previously published as *Rudolph's Second Christmas*

ISBN-13: 978-0-439-93318-6
ISBN-10: 0-439-93318-8

12 11 10 9 8 7 6   6 7 8 9 10 11/0

Printed in the U.S.A.   40

First Scholastic printing, December 2006

Rudolph
to the Rescue

By Robert L. May
Illustrated by Lisa Papp

SCHOLASTIC INC.
New York Toronto London Auckland Sydney
Mexico City New Delhi Hong Kong Buenos Aires

Remember Rudolph the Red-Nosed Reindeer's first exciting Christmas? Remember how his red, shining nose showed Santa the way through the dark and foggy Christmas Eve sky?

Well, when Santa and Rudolph finally finished leaving all the boys and girls their presents that night, they were both *so* tired that they went away for a long rest. (Rudolph, of course, first asked his Mother and Daddy if he could go.)

North Po

So that no one would be able to find them or bother them, they went as *far* from Santa's North Pole office as they could . . . way down to the South Pole.

After a three-week rest, Santa took Rudolph back to his Mother and Daddy. Then Santa went back to his own North Pole office.

He unlocked the front door and pushed, but the door hardly budged. Then he backed up, took a running start, and crashed his big, round tummy against the door, just as hard as he could. Santa bounced off, like a big round rubber ball. The door moved a little this time, just enough for Santa to squeeze in.

And there he found the whole room filled
to the ceiling with letters the mailman had
dropped through the mail-slot while Santa'd
been away . . . letters written by children to
thank Santa for their presents.
"How will I *ever* be able to read them?" cried
Santa. "With just one small lamp in my
office, and the North Pole night six months
long, I'll ruin my eyes.

"If only Rudolph were here to help me, and to light up the room with his shining red nose! *There's* an idea! I'll phone him." So Santa sent for Rudolph, who came right away, sat down next to Santa, and helped him open and read those piles and piles of letters.

Suddenly, Santa heard . . . Rudolph was crying . . .
"Here, Santa, you read this letter,
before my tears make the words any wetter."

Dear Santa,

You didn't find us, Christmas Eve, because Daddy's circus moves to a different town every day so our stockings were empty Christmas morning.

We didn't get any presents at all. Please, Santa, try hard to find us next Christmas, cause Mother and Daddy say we've been very, very good.

with
LOVE,
SONNY
and Sis

Then Rudolph said to Santa:
"We'll have to find out where their circus will be.
And the very best person to find them . . . is me!"

So Rudolph traveled to the town where Sonny and Sis's letter had been mailed. Meeting some boys and girls, Rudolph asked if they knew where the circus was.

"That silly little circus? It left for the next town *weeks* ago."

"It only stayed here one day."

"Nobody went to see it."

"It was *terrible*."

The same thing happened in the next town. And the next. And the next. And, ten towns later, when Rudolph finally caught up with "that silly little circus," he quickly understood why *no* town would let it stay for more than one day.

The circus band, instead of playing the
way circus bands *should* . . . played like this:
Bzzz! Bzzz! Bzzz!
Clank! Clank! Clank! Clank!
Booop! Booop! Tooot!
B-B-B-Bash! C-C-C-Crash! B-B-Bash! C-C-Crash!
R-R-R-R-R-R-R-R-R-R!
Ting-a-ling! Ting-a-ling!
Ching-a! Ching-a! Ching!

Instead of lions and tigers that roared real loud . . .
they had just one toothless old tiger who didn't
scare *anyone*. And instead of shooting a man from
a cannon, they shot a tiny mouse from a popgun.

"No wonder no one buys tickets,"
Sonny said sadly to Rudolph.
"By next Christmas, Rudolph," cried Sis, "we don't
know *where* we'll be! So you and Santa may not find us
next Christmas, either."
You can easily see why Rudolph felt sadder than ever when he left
Sonny and Sis and the circus and started his long trip back to the
North Pole.

That evening, while going through a dark forest and looking for a place to sleep, Rudolph heard noises he felt quite sure must be animals. . . . When Rudolph got close enough to shine his red nose on them, was he surprised!

The sound of an animal running very fast . . . was a
turtle . . . another walking very, very slowly . . . a rabbit!
The barking came from a cat . . . the meows from a dog.
The singing bird was a parrot . . . and the talking bird
was a canary. (And *none* of them looked very happy.)
Rudolph looked at the animals and said:
"You all look so sad, and you all look so queer. . . .
Excuse me for staring . . . but why are you here?"

"I'm the best talker here," the canary said to Rudolph. "So I'll try to tell you why we're here. You can't really *expect* us to look happy. After all, each of us has been stared at and laughed at and teased, ever since we were babies. Just because we're a little different from other animals we used to live with.

"Take *me*: when I couldn't learn to sing like the other canaries, no matter how *hard* I tried, but could only talk instead, the others all made fun of me. So when I grew up, I left them and flew away to a different forest. And here I am."

Rudolph then learned from the canary how the parrot had come to this forest for almost the same reason—it had never learned to say "Polly want a cracker," like the smarter parrots, but could only just sing.

The dog that said "meow" had been teased and barked at by the rest of the dogs.

Because the barking cat sounded just like a dog, she couldn't help frightening all the other cats, who would run up the nearest tree when they heard her.

The slow-walking rabbit could never keep up with his fast-moving friends. And whenever the fast-running turtle tried to slow up to wait for the others, he would trip and land on his back. (And you probably know how hard it is for an upside-down turtle to get on his *feet* again!)

So each of these little animals had been sad and lonely, laughed at and teased. Even after they had all come together in the forest, they were still a little sad and a little lonesome. (But at least they didn't tease or laugh at each other. After all, there was *something* a bit peculiar about *each* of them!)

"As a matter of fact," the canary said to Rudolph, "you're a little
different from other reindeer, too! Why don't you stay here with us?
After all, isn't your nose a little bit, er . . . a little, er . . ."
Rudolph smiled and said,
"You can't hurt my feelings; my nose is a sight.
But it sure helped old Santa, that dark, foggy night!
I know how it feels to be teased just like you,
But I've an idea. I know what I'll do
To make each of you just as happy as me.
So first I'll tell Santa. Then, boy! Wait and see."

Can you guess what Rudolph's wonderful idea was?

Yes, by Christmas that year, the "silly little circus" had become the grandest in the whole wide world! All because of Rudolph's idea . . .

YOU WON'T BELIEVE YOUR EARS!!
the BAFFLING and
BEWILDERING...
BARKING CAT!!!

MEOWS! TRUE!

TALKING CANARY!

Sonny and Sis's parents were happy, because they had a circus everyone wanted to see. All the boys and girls were so happy to see this great circus that it wasn't able to leave the town for ten whole months. Santa and Rudolph were happy, too, because they knew that this year they would have no trouble finding Sonny and Sis and filling their stockings all the way to the top.

Sonny and Sis were happy, because this year Santa brought them everything they asked for.
In fact, he brought each of them an extra present because of having missed them the year before.

And when it was all over, Santa said, "Rudolph, you've made as many people happy on this, your second Christmas with me, as you did on your first."

Rudolph felt very proud, and he said . . .
"I hope you'll invite me to help you each year.
The happiest moment allowed any deer
Is riding with you, sir, and guiding your sleigh
(The number-one job on the number-one day)
And calling to all, as we drive out of sight—

"MERRY CHRISTMAS TO ALL,
AND TO ALL A GOOD NIGHT!"